W9-CKH-586

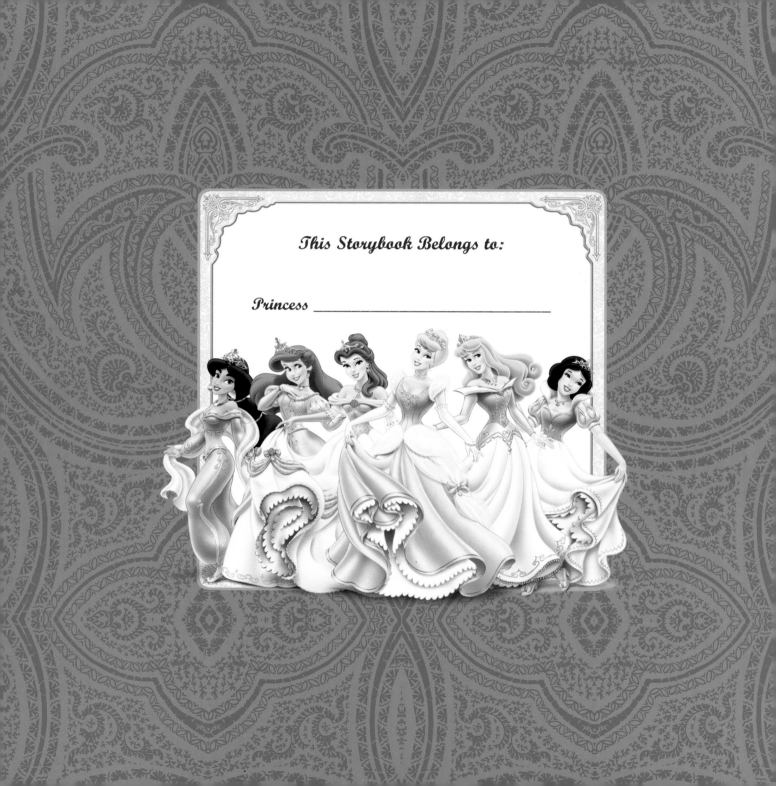

This Storybook Belongs to:

Princess _____

Disney Princess

Sleeping Beauty

Enchanted Moments

ADVANCE PUBLISHERS

Once upon a time, in a faraway land, there lived King Stefan and his queen who held a great feast to celebrate the birth of their daughter, Aurora.

King Hubert of a nearby kingdom and his young son, Phillip, were guests at the feast. The two kings made plans for Prince Phillip and Princess Aurora to marry on Aurora's sixteenth birthday.

Three good fairies, Flora, Fauna, and Merryweather, also attended the party. Each of them brought a special gift.

Flora gave the princess the gift of beauty. Fauna gave the princess the gift of song.

Finally, Merryweather approached the cradle. Before she could offer her gift, a loud boom of thunder announced the arrival of Maleficent, the wicked fairy. She was very angry that she had not been invited to the feast.

Maleficent looked down at the sleeping infant. "I also have a gift for you," she began. "Before the sun sets on your sixteenth birthday, you will prick your finger on the spindle of a spinning wheel and die!"

When Maleficent left, Merryweather tried to calm the terrified crowd. "I still have my gift for the princess," she reminded everyone.

Raising her magic wand, the good fairy whispered, "Not in death, but just in sleep, the fateful prophecy you will keep. And from this slumber, you shall wake, when true love's kiss the spell shall break."

King Stefan still worried about Aurora's safety. He ordered every spinning wheel in the kingdom to be destroyed.

Then, the good fairies came up with a plan. They told the king and queen that they would disguise themselves as peasants and raise the child deep in the forest. When the curse ended on Aurora's sixteenth birthday, they would all return to the castle.

The king and queen reluctantly agreed.

Flora, Fauna, and Merryweather gave Aurora a new name: Briar Rose. They took her far into the woods to live in a little cottage. There, the fairies put away their magic wands so that Maleficent would never find them or Aurora.

As the years passed, Maleficent and her henchmen kept searching for the princess, but she was never found.

Finally, the wicked fairy sent her pet raven out to search. "Oh, my pet," said Maleficent. "You are my last hope. Circle far and wide. Search for a maiden with hair of sunshine gold and lips red as a rose. Go, and do not fail me!"

On the morning of Briar Rose's sixteenth birthday, the good fairies sent her out to collect berries so they could prepare her birthday surprise.

After gathering the berries, Briar Rose rested in the glade. She sang about her wish to fall in love with a handsome prince. Her friends, the animals and birds, listened happily.

Meanwhile, Prince Phillip had been riding through the woods on his horse, Samson. Phillip heard the beautiful voice in the trees and took off to find the singer.

Samson galloped along and, as he jumped over a log, the prince was thrown into a pond. He set his wet clothes out to dry.

Moments later, without the prince seeing them, the animals brought a cape, hat, and boots to Briar Rose. They dressed up as her make-believe prince and danced with her.

Prince Phillip followed the voice and discovered the beautiful maiden. He and Briar Rose fell in love at first sight.

But when the prince asked her name, Briar Rose remembered that the fairies had told her never to talk to strangers. When it was time for Briar Rose to go, she invited him to visit her cottage that evening.

Meanwhile, the three fairies were having a difficult time with their party preparations. Fauna made a lopsided birthday cake. Flora and Merryweather had made a special dress for Briar Rose, but something about it just didn't look quite right.

The good fairies needed a touch of magic to help them. So they agreed to use their wands—just this once.

Before trying out their wands, the good fairies blocked every opening in the cottage. They had to stop any magic dust from escaping and revealing their secret hideaway. But someone forgot to block the chimney!

Maleficent's raven flew by just as some magic streamed out of the cottage chimney. At last, the raven had found the princess! He raced back to the Forbidden Mountains to tell Maleficent.

By the time Briar Rose returned to the cottage, the party was ready. She thanked Flora, Fauna, and Merryweather for the beautiful new dress and delicious cake. "This is the happiest day of my life," she said.

Then she told them about the handsome stranger she had met in the woods. "I invited him to come here this evening," she explained.

The fairies realized that Briar Rose had fallen in love. "It's time we told her the truth," said Fauna sadly.

Briar Rose learned that she was really a princess who was betrothed to a prince named Phillip. "I'm sorry, child," said Flora. "Tonight we're taking you back to your parents, the king and queen."

As soon as darkness fell, the good fairies led a sad Briar Rose through the forest to the castle. As she walked, Briar Rose could only think of her handsome stranger.

At the castle, Flora, Fauna, and Merryweather left Aurora in a quiet room to rest. Suddenly, a strange glowing light appeared. Aurora followed it in a trance-like state. It led her up a winding staircase to an attic room. Inside the room was Maleficent—waiting by a spinning wheel.

Aurora reached out. She pricked her finger on the spindle and fell to the floor.

As soon as the good fairies discovered Aurora, they cast a spell over the kingdom, putting everyone to sleep. This would save the king and queen from heartbreak and give the good fairies time to find Aurora's true love. Only true love's kiss could break the spell.

Between snores, the fairies heard King Hubert mention something about his son, Prince Phillip, wanting to marry a peasant girl.

The fairies realized that Briar Rose's stranger must be the prince! They hurried back to the cottage to find him.

But they were too late. Maleficent had captured Prince Phillip and was keeping him prisoner in her dungeon.

The good fairies went to Maleficent's dungeon and freed the prince. Then they gave him the magical Shield of Virtue and the Sword of Truth.

Prince Phillip used the sword to cut his way through a forest of thorns.
There, he came upon Maleficent who had turned herself into a fierce and terrible
dragon. But the dragon was no match for Phillip and the Sword of Truth.

After slaying the dragon, Phillip raced back to the castle and found Aurora. Kneeling down beside her, he kissed her gently. The princess awakened with a smile.

Flying about, the good fairies woke up everyone in the kingdom. And that night, the prince and his princess danced happily in each other's arms.